To: _____

From: _____

Big Sister, Little Sister

story and pictures by **Marci Curtis**

DIAL BOOKS FOR YOUNG READERS **NEW YORK**

Rodney Curtis

To Skye and Taylor—best sisters, best daughters, best friends.

Thousands of thanks to Nzingha, Sandile, Catherine, Elizabeth, Tiler, Makala,
and their families for sharing their sisterly love.

Published by Dial Books for Young Readers
A division of Penguin Putnam Inc.
345 Hudson Street
New York, New York 10014

Copyright © 2000 by Marci Curtis
Designed by Kimi Weart
Manufactured in China on acid-free paper
1 3 5 7 9 10 8 6 4 2

Library of Congress Cataloging in Publication Data
Curtis, Marci.
Big sister, little sister/story and pictures by Marci Curtis.—1st ed.
p.   cm.
Summary: Photo illustrations of real-life sisters
accompanied by a rhyming description of sisterhood.
ISBN 0-8037-2482-9 (hardcover)
[1. Sisters—Fiction. 2. Stories in rhyme.] I. Title.
PZ8.3.C93445Bi   2000
[E]—dc21   99-24796   CIP
Special Markets ISBN 0-8037-3131-0
Not For Resale

Big Sister, Little Sister, a love that is so strong.
Big Sister, Little Sister, best friends all year long.

Big Sister and I, *racing* hand in hand.

Little Sister picks the **biggest** pumpkin in the land.

Big Sister shows me how to *yell* **and** Cheer!

"Little Sister, it's okay. I will dry your tear."

Big Sister swipes a bite. "Don't be such a pig!"

"Little Sister, please let go and I'll buy you a wig."

Big Sister shows me how to brush my smile.

Little Sister gives the dog a super- silly **style.**

Big Sister teaches me to .

Little Sister follows where I *lead*.

Big Sister takes a sip from my gigantic drink.

"Little Sister, eat some sn❄w. It's very clean . . . I think."

Big Sister and I, ZIPPED UP two-in-one.

Little Sister learns how *homework* is done.

Big Sister shares her musical gift.

"Little Sister, you can reach—with a little lift."

Big Sister teaches me the sign for "I l♥ve y♥u."

"Little Sister, heels are tricky, especially when you're two."

Big Sister *soars* **with me on a rainy day.**

Little Sister wants to know, "*Now* who's going to play?"

Big Sister's **TANTRUMS** always make me cry.

Little Sister cracks up—and so do I!

Big Sister helps me draw a chalky **fantasy.**

Little Sister makes a sandy angel out of me.

Big Sister plays a game of hide-and-seek.

Little Sister's bubble 'do is oh so very chic.

Big Sister loves to comb and braid my hair.

Little Sister skips **with me. We make a** springy **pair!**

Big Sister, Little Sister, best forever friends.
Big and Little Sister, a love that never ends.